For Mitch, Ken, David, and even Debbie —S.L.
For Wilma and Hannelore —M.L.

No part of this publication may be reproduced, stored in a retrieval system, or transmitted in any form or by any means, electronic, mechanical, photocopying, recording, or otherwise, without written permission of the publisher. For information regarding permission, write to Random House Children's Books, a division of Penguin Random House LLC, Permissions Department, 1745 Broadway, 15th Floor, New York, NY 10019.

ISBN 978-1-338-89461-5

Text copyright © 2020 by Suzanne Lang. Cover art and interior illustrations copyright © 2020 by Max Lang. All rights reserved. Published by Scholastic Inc., 557 Broadway, New York, NY 10012, by arrangement with Random House Children's Books, a division of Penguin Random House LLC. GRUMPY MONKEY is a registered trademark of Pick & Flick Pictures, Inc. SCHOLASTIC and associated logos are trademarks and/or registered trademarks of Scholastic Inc.

12 11 10 9 8 7 6 5 4 3 2 1   23 24 25 26 27 28

Printed in the U.S.A.   40

First Scholastic printing, January 2023

GRUMPY MONKEY
UP ALL NIGHT

By Suzanne Lang

Illustrated by Max Lang

SCHOLASTIC INC.

Early in the evening—just about suppertime—Norman heard a whole lot of whooping and hollering next door.

"What's the ruckus?" Norman asked his neighbor Jim Panzee.

"I'm so excited!" Jim exclaimed. "I'm going to a sleepover at my parents' house!"

"My whole family will be there! Mom, Dad, and my big sisters, Ann and Nan!"

"Who's that?" asked Norman.

"Oh yeah. My little brother, Tim," grumbled Jim.
"But never mind. It'll still be fun."
"Sleepovers are a good time," Norman agreed.

Jim talked about all the great things he would do.

"First we'll go termite fishing."

"Next we'll tell scary stories."

"Then we'll have a midnight feast."

"And wash it down
with some jungle punch."

"I wouldn't drink punch too close to bedtime," Norman advised.

"Bedtime?!" exclaimed Jim. "Nobody sleeps at a sleepover! We're going to stay up all night!"

"Sounds fun," said Norman. "Mind if I tag along?"

A little later, they arrived at the tree
where Jim's parents lived.

"It's my little Grumpy Monkey!" Jim's mom
cried as she gave him a hug. "I'm so happy to see you!"

"Mom!" moaned Jim. "I'm NOT little! And I'm not a
monkey! I'm an ape!"

Jim's mom smiled and ruffled his fur.
"But you sure are grumpy!" she said.
"No, I'm not!" Jim scowled.
"I like your mom," said Norman.

"No fair! You didn't say we could bring a friend!" said a voice coming down the path.

"Who's that?" asked Norman.

"Tim!" exclaimed Jim's family.

"I thought you said he was your *little* brother," said Norman.

"I had a growth spurt," said Tim.

"What should we do first?" asked Jim's mom.

Everyone answered at once.

"Termite fishing!"

"Pick fleas off each other!"

"Bob for mangoes!"

"I know," said Tim. "Measure each other to see who's tallest!"

"Maybe our guest should choose," suggested Jim's dad, turning to Norman.

"It's a tough decision," said Norman. "It all sounds fun."

"Don't worry," said Ann. "There'll be plenty of time to do everything because we're going to stay—"

"UP ALL NIGHT!" cheered Jim and his siblings.

"I don't know," said Jim's mom. "Staying up all night could make for some very grumpy monkeys."

And then the games began.

TERMITE FISHING

SCARY STORIES

"It was a dark and stormy night," said Jim.
Tim trembled.

"Your brother's scared," said
Jim's mom. "Why not tell a happy
story instead?"

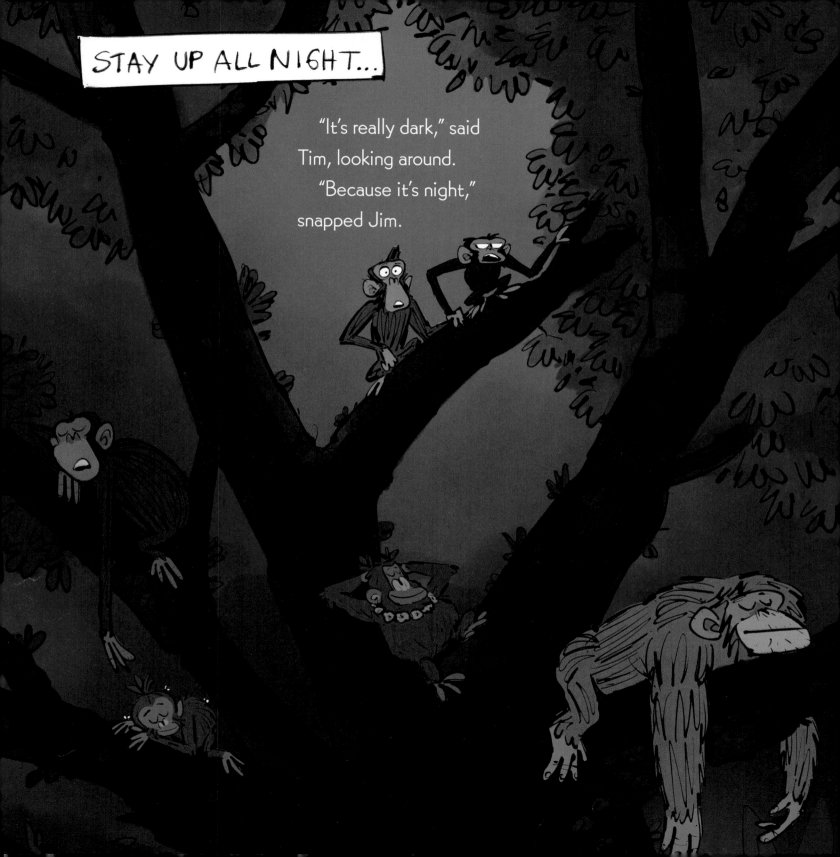

STAY UP ALL NIGHT...

"It's really dark," said
Tim, looking around.
"Because it's night,"
snapped Jim.

"Are you grumpy?" asked Tim.
"No!" said Jim.
Just then they heard a noise.

RAAAAA

"Thunder!" shouted Tim, and his eyes went wide. "Oh no, now it's dark *and* stormy."

"Don't worry," said Jim. "It's just Norman snoring. He does lots of funny snores. Sometimes it sounds like *raa-raa-raa-raa*, and sometimes it sounds like *prfffffprffffffprffff*." Tim laughed. "Other times it's like *haaaaWEEEEEhaaaaWEEEEE*!"

Jim and Tim laughed and laughed all night long.

As the sun came up, Tim fell asleep.
"Good idea, little brother," said Jim as he
tucked Tim in and lay down.

But just as he was about
to close his eyes . . .

"Good morning, my monkeys!" sang Jim's mom.

"Mom!" shouted Jim. "We're not monkeys! We're apes!"

"I prefer 'gorilla,' but yeah, 'ape' works," said Norman.

"Oh, Jim, I told you staying up all night would make
you grumpy," said Jim's mom, ruffling his fur.

"I'M NOT—"

"You'll always be my Grumpy Monkey,"
whispered Jim's mom.